# BLAST FROM
# THE PAST

by Karen Stamfil
illustrated by Barbara Higgins Bond

## Chapters

**Harcourt**

Orlando   Boston   Dallas   Chicago   San Diego

Visit *The Learning Site!*

www.harcourtschool.com

## Old Is Good

As far as Jason was concerned, *this* was the start of the vacation. For two weeks he and his parents had been seeing the sights of Europe. They had saved and planned for years to make the trip. Now they were in the Greek islands. This was the place Jason most wanted to visit.

"Look there." Jason's father pointed to a high stone arch. "Is that old enough to make you happy?"

"Not really," Jason said. "It's a Roman aqueduct. It's probably no more than 2,000 years old."

Still, the huge arch was impressive. Jason knew that the Romans had built the aqueducts to bring water from mountain springs into the cities. An aqueduct was made up of a series of these huge arches. It stretched for many miles.

The arches supported an overhead canal. The canal was made of stone blocks. Water flowed from the mountains, through the canals, all the way to the cities.

When his family had visited Rome, Jason had seen many aqueducts. A total of 24 aqueducts had brought water to Rome.

Now the aqueducts were beginning to crumble. Still, they weren't very old, in Jason's opinion.

## A Dig Nearby

Jason was delighted to find that there was an archaeological dig not far from their hotel. After lunch he went down there for a look.

The archaeologist in charge was a Professor Diaz. She was from a university in the United States. She didn't seem to mind answering Jason's questions.

"You seem to know a lot about ancient Greece," she said. "Yes, we've found some interesting things. This mosaic dates from the third century A.D. Look here. Luke just cleaned the emblem of the artist who made it."

Jason saw that the mosaic was made from pebbles that had been worn smooth by water. The artist had found pebbles of different colors and placed them so they formed a picture of a lion.

"Were all the mosaics made from pebbles back then?" he asked.

"Most artists used pebbles in the third century," the professor told him. "After that, they started using cubes cut from stone and glass. The cubes allowed them to make more complicated designs."

"Have you found anything from classical Greece?" Jason asked. He knew that during their classical period, the Greeks had produced their best art, architecture, and drama. The classical period took place during the fifth century B.C. Athens and Sparta were separate states then, and they were at war with each other.

"We've found quite a lot from that period," said Professor Diaz. "We've uncovered Athenian coins, household items, and hardware from ships. In fact, this island was an Athenian colony. The street we're standing on dates from around 450 B.C. The drain in the middle was for public hygiene."

"We're hoping to find some Minoan artifacts," the professor continued.

Jason knew from his reading that the Minoans had lived on the Greek island of Crete long ago.

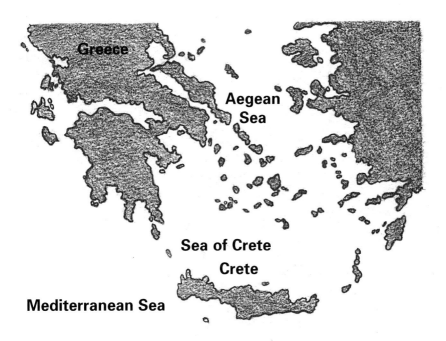

Greece

Aegean Sea

Sea of Crete

Crete

Mediterranean Sea

"My guess is that the Minoans were here, but Luke, Lydia, Paul, and I haven't proved it yet." Professor Diaz smiled. "I hope we do, and soon. Then the university would pay for five more years of digging."

Paul was digging nearby. "It would be wonderful to be able to work here for five more years," he said.

## No Sale

Later, Jason and his parents walked through the town. Jason talked about Professor Diaz.

"That would really be something if she found Minoan stuff," he said. "The Minoans lived 3,700 years ago. They built incredible palaces and created great works of art. They even knew about personal hygiene. They had sewers thousands of years before anyone else."

"Look." Jason's father pointed to a shop near the Roman aqueduct. "Want to have a look?"

The shop sold antiquities of all kinds. There were tools and pottery, sculpture and writing tablets.

"Do you see anything you like?" the shop-keeper asked in English.

"Not really," Jason said. The only things he could afford were some coins with the emblem of the Roman emperor Titus. But he already had enough coins in his collection. "You've got some interesting stuff, though. Is it all from this island?"

"Oh, no," said the shopkeeper. "People bring me things from all over." She pointed to a small pot. "This was found on the island of Kos. And this mosaic is from a Roman estate in Thrace. Or was it Achaea? Oh, well, it was one of the provinces of the Roman Empire."

That's the trouble with shops like this, Jason thought to himself. They'll buy and sell anything. They don't care where it comes from, or when it was made. It's hard to reconstruct the past if you don't leave things in place. That's the only way they can be studied properly.

"Thanks for the information. I guess I should be going," Jason said to the shopkeeper as he walked toward the door.

Just as Jason was leaving, Paul entered the shop and bumped into Jason.

"Oh, excuse me," Jason said.

"That's okay," Paul said as he hurried into the store.

"Hmm," Jason thought. "I guess he's in as big a hurry as I am to reconstruct the past."

# Excitement at the Site

The next day Jason and his parents took a boat ride around the island. As they cruised back into the harbor, Jason saw lots of people and cars crowding around the archaeological site.

"That looks like a TV truck," he said.

"And that helicopter has a government emblem," his mother said.

There was a lot of excitement around the dig.
Work seemed to have stopped. Professor Diaz was
speaking in Greek to a TV reporter. When she
recognized Jason, she smiled and waved.

"You brought us good luck!" the professor said.
"Lydia here turned up a Minoan artifact this
morning. Paul called the Antiquities Ministry in
Athens. This is Dr. Pappas. She's an expert the
government sends out to the provinces to check
on archaeological findings."

"It certainly looks authentic," said Dr. Pappas.
"Of course, we can't be sure until we've run some
tests."

Luke showed Jason the artifact. It was a bronze sculpture, still half-buried in sand.

"This is very exciting," Luke said. "You see this image over and over in Minoan art. And it's right at the level where you'd expect to find something Minoan. Sometimes we find an artifact where it has no right to be—like a thousand years too early. Then we have a mystery on our hands."

Jason looked at the sculpture. Why did it look so familiar? He thought about the people he had met at the dig. And he thought about other things he had seen on the island.

"They do have a mystery on their hands!" Jason thought.

Professor Diaz was still talking to Dr. Pappas. "Excuse me," Jason said. "You may have a problem. Before you make an official report, you may want to check out a few things."

The professor said something in Greek to the official. Then Dr. Pappas turned to Jason.

"Dr. Diaz said not to be fooled by how young you are," she said in English. "She says you know a lot about archaeology. So you think you've spotted a fake?"

"Not a fake—a plant," Jason said. "I think someone buried that Minoan artifact there so it would be found. Here's why..."

*Who is the person that Jason suspects? And why does Jason suspect that person?*